Biscuit Loves Mother's Day

story by ALYSSA SATIN CAPUCILLI
pictures by PAT SCHORIES

HarperFestival®
A Division of HarperCollins*Publishers*

"Come along, Biscuit.
Today is Mother's Day.
Mother's Day is a great day to show Mom how much we care."

Woof, woof!

"This picture will be a perfect present for Mom, Biscuit."

Woof, woof!

"Wait, Biscuit!"

"There are lots of ways to celebrate Mother's Day, Biscuit. Today, we'll surprise Mom with breakfast in bed! Chocolate chip pancakes are her favorite."

Woof, woof!

"Mom loves to garden, Biscuit.
We can help with the planting and watering."

Woof, woof!

"The sun is shining. There's hardly a cloud in the sky. It's a wonderful day for a bicycle ride!"

Woof, woof!

"Biscuit, where are you going?"

"Here, Biscuit.
It's time for Dad to set up the picnic blanket."

Woof, woof!

"Look!
Even the ducks are celebrating Mother's Day."

Woof, woof!
Quack! Quack!

"There's nothing better than spending the day with Mom, is there, Biscuit?
Happy Mother's Day, Mom. We love you."

Woof!